K

Kachunka! The magical powers of this out-of-this-world dinner lady are not to be sneezed at!

Enid Richemont was born and brought up in Wales. She studied at Dublin College of Art and then wrote short stories for magazines before starting her own design business, producing play equipment for children. She began writing stories to entertain her own children and their friends. In 1989 Walker Books published her first title, *The Time Tree*. She has since written several other books, including three other stories for young readers, *The Glass Bird*, *The Magic Skateboard* and *Gemma and the Beetle People*.

Some other titles

Change the King!
by Hugh Scott

The Green Kids
by Sam McBratney

The Human Zoo
by Virginia Ironside

Jake's Magic
by Alan Durant

Kid Kibble
by Diana Hendry

The Magic Skateboard
by Enid Richemont

Second-time Charley
by Kathy Henderson

Stone Croc
by Penelope Farmer

KACHUNKA!

Enid Richemont

Illustrations by
Margaret Chamberlain

WALKER BOOKS
LONDON

For David, with love

First published 1992 by Walker Books Ltd
87 Vauxhall Walk, London SE11 5HJ

Text © 1992 Enid Richemont
Illustrations © 1992 Margaret Chamberlain

This edition published 1993

Printed in England by Clays Ltd, St Ives plc

British Library Cataloguing in Publication Data
A catalogue record for this book
is available from the British Library.

ISBN 0-7445-3100-4

CONTENTS

Chapter One

Class Five had just lined up when the woman unlatched the gate and walked across the playground.

People turned to watch her. It would have been difficult not to. Even the caretaker's cat stiffened and nosed at the air.

Class Five began muttering, "Who's she? Who's she?"

Simon shrugged and tapped his forehead. "Some loony..."

"Bet she's a clown," said Amanda. "Hope she comes to us."

"Hope she doesn't," said Simon. "Boring. Boring."

Miss Fielding frowned. "Come on, you lot," she said. "Manners. It's rude to stare – you know that."

"But she's got blue hair!" shouted Thomas.

"S-s-sh," hissed Miss Fielding. "Maybe she likes it that way. Maybe you'll dye yours blue one day…"

Thomas touched his pale, untidy fuzz. "No I won't," he said loudly. "My dad wouldn't let me."

Simon groaned. "Your dad, your dad…"

"That's enough," said Miss Fielding. "Let's go in."

Amanda turned and pointed. "Look! Snowball likes her…"

"So what?" said Simon.

In the corner of the playground, the woman was speaking to the head dinner lady.

"I saw your notice," she was saying, tucking a braid of sea-blue hair under an orange wool cap.

"What notice?" said Mrs Harries warily.

"About needing extra help…"

The woman smiled down at the white cat who was now sniffing delicately around the hem of her skirt.

"Oh yes," said Mrs Harries, staring at the strange green bloom on the visitor's plum-brown skin.

"I can help with school dinners…"

"Oh yes," said Mrs Harries, frowning at the frayed and dangling lining of the baggy tweed coat.

"And with playground duty…"

Mrs Harries watched with distaste as Snowball rose and rubbed herself against the woman's lumpy canvas boots.

"And school trips…"

"Got references, have you?" said Mrs Harries suspiciously. "Worked with children before?"

"With all kinds of beings…" The woman smiled and held out her hand, enclosing Mrs Harries' cold pink fingers in a warm, furry grasp. "Kachunka," she announced.

"Bless you!" grumbled Mrs Harries.

"*Mrs* Kachunka."

Mrs Harries quickly withdrew her hand. "Oh, pardon me, I'm sure."

Then Mrs Harries counted. She counted again to check.

"Too many," she said.

"Oh, not for me," said the woman. "I can cope. I like children…"

"Fingers," said Mrs Harries, pointing.

"Oh those…" And the woman spread her russet-green hands.

Mrs Harries stepped hurriedly backwards. She could clearly count fourteen downy fingers, each one tipped with an ivory point. Wasn't natural, she thought. Wasn't right.

Mrs Kachunka smiled. "And you have…?"

"Ten," said Mrs Harries firmly. "Like everyone else."

"Oh dear," said Mrs Kachunka.

Mrs Harries looked down at her own hands. "So what's wrong with ten?"

"So few."

Mrs Harries coughed. This was getting ridiculous.

"Are you one of our parents?" she demanded.

The small whiskers on Mrs Kachunka's downy cheeks twitched with amusement.

"Do I look like one of your parents?"

"Can't say that you do," said Mrs Harries gruffly. She was beginning to feel cross. Someone was trying to make a fool out of her. Well she wasn't having any. No one could make a fool out of Mrs Harries...

Blue hair? Had to be a wig. Green whiskers? Stuck on with some kind of glue. And those extra fingers? Plastic, probably. You could buy things like that in joke shops.

"You're one of them actors, aren't you?" she said disapprovingly. "That's what you are. Didn't fool me though ... not for one minute." She sniffed. "I'll take you to see Mr Carey. Got an appointment, have you?"

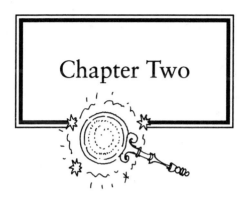

Chapter Two

Mrs Harries tapped politely at the open door.

Mr Carey was just finishing his cup of tea.

Mrs Harries jerked her thumb at Mrs Kachunka. "Someone to see you."

Mr Carey looked up. "Good heavens," he said.

Snowball was standing on her hind legs, making dough against Mrs Kachunka's coat. Mrs Harries clapped her hands. "Shoo!" she said. "Shoo!"

Mr Carey put on his spectacles and reached for his timetable. Clown? he wondered. Actor? Storyteller? But for which class? He cleared his throat.

"Thank you, Mrs Harries…"

Mrs Kachunka walked up to the desk. "Kachunka," she said.

"Bless you!" said Mr Carey.

"*Mrs* Kachunka."

"Ah, yes. Quite so. Yes." Mr Carey pulled himself together. "And you've come to visit Class…?"

"I've come to help."

Mr Carey coughed. "In what way?" he probed delicately.

"I saw your notice," said Mrs Kachunka. "You need helpers. Volunteers. For dinners and playground duty and school trips."

Mr Carey looked embarrassed. "We really meant relatives. Parents. People we know…" He peered at her. "*Do* we know you?"

Mrs Kachunka took a small silver lozenge out of her coat pocket and popped it into her mouth. "Lunchtime," she explained.

"Quite so," said Mr Carey.

Then Mrs Kachunka brought out a large eyeglass with a mirrored handle.

"Do sit down," said Mr Carey nervously. Her right eye, through the greenish crystal, seemed to grow and grow. Surely nobody's eyes could be that shade of turquoise? Surely nobody's eyes should have a slit in the middle, like a little shutter?

The shutter slowly opened.

"Oh!" gasped Mr Carey. "Oh…" And galaxies went spinning around his head. "Stop!" he yelled. "I'm getting giddy…"

"*Nothing stops*," said a voice. "*Not even you…*"

Then Mr Carey went spiralling round a million suns.

"This is the life!" he sang. "No more teaching! No more school…"

Then Mr Carey turned into a round planet with a moon for an eye and a star for a crown. Mountains and rivers rose out of his back and trees and flowers grew out of his head. "*You see, Mr Carey?*" the voice said. "*You are everything. Everything…*"

Wings grew between Mr Carey's shoulders and he settled in a tree. He was an owl, then a bear, then a squirrel, then a mouse. I should take notes, he thought, for my Nature classes.

He was a beetle, a worm, a flea, an atom. "*Everything…*"

"Yes, I see," muttered Mr Carey. "And you've come to observe … us?" He blinked. "Why, of course we know you," he said vaguely. "Glad to have you with us, Mrs er…" and he counted the fingers on one of Mrs Kachunka's hands – one, two, three, four, five, six, seven. A useful number, thought Mr Carey, curling his own five around the handle of the teapot. "Would you care for a cup?"

By the end of that week, everyone was talking about the new school helper.

"She dyes her hair."

"She's got a green moustache."

"She eats those silver things…"

"And nothing else."

"She's got too many fingers."

"Don't know why we have to have her," grumbled Mrs Harries. "More trouble than she's worth."

For Mrs Kachunka
put boiled carrots into
rice pudding.
"Pretty," she said,
arranging them in
a ring.

She poured yellow
custard over fried liver
and put a cherry on
top of each helping.
"Yuk!" they
all said.

She scattered
chocolate sprinkles
over fish pie and
stirred strawberry
jam into baked beans.

The children giggled and said, "You've
got it all wrong again, Mrs Kachunka!"

But on Friday Mrs Kachunka turned up
with a large cold bag full of ice lollies.

"Bad for their teeth," said Mrs Harries.

"Oh, just this once," begged Mrs Kachunka. "I made so many mistakes."

Mrs Harries banged saucepans and rattled plates.

"Always messing things up," she grumbled. "I don't hold with them theatricals. Why can't they be like everyone else? Lot of silly nonsense, that's what I call it."

"Our new dinner lady's a nutcase," Simon said to his mum.

"You say everyone's a nutcase," yawned Simon's mum. "Nothing new about that."

Anna told her mum, "Listen. She puts curry on our ice-cream."

"Then scrape it off," said Anna's mum, turning a page of her magazine.

Lalita told her dad who said, "Big girls like you don't make up such stories."

But Thomas didn't tell anyone.

Chapter Three

Theodora told her aunt, who said, "How dreadful! We'll complain."

"Oh don't do that," begged Theodora.

Her aunt ignored her.

"Dyed hair? Green whiskers? Where *does* the woman come from? And that awful name! Sounds just like a sneeze."

Theodora giggled. "I know."

On Monday afternoon Theodora's aunt took Theodora firmly by the hand and marched her back into school. The school secretary was tidying up.

"I have a complaint," announced Theodora's aunt.

The school secretary sighed. "Mrs Kachunka?"

Theodora's aunt swelled up like a balloon, until her violet jacket looked as if it might burst every one of its buttons.

"It ought not to be allowed," she said.

"She's beginning to get the hang of things now," said the school secretary, who rather liked Mrs Kachunka. "I wouldn't worry if I were you."

"But you're *not* me," declared Theodora's aunt, and her heavy gold rings seemed to glitter with outrage. "My niece will be bringing sandwiches from now on."

"Oh, not sandwiches," grumbled Theodora. "Boring…"

Thomas was already bringing sandwiches. On Monday morning he'd secretly slipped his dinner money back into his mum's purse and popped a small wedge of dry cheese between two pieces of sliced bread.

That lunchtime, Mrs Kachunka topped each helping of chocolate pudding with a sugared almond.

"Oooh," they said. "Mrs Kachunka – you've got it right this time!"

Then she swept over to the people who brought packed lunches and set down ten sugared almonds in a ring, like a pale spring flower.

"I saved them for you."

"Oooh," they yelled. "Thank you, Mrs Kachunka!"

"I wouldn't touch them," said Thomas, knocking over Carly's orange juice. "She's nuts. They're probably poisoned."

"*You're* nuts, you mean," said Carly, wiping juice from her jumper. "Look what you've just done!"

"Don't you want yours?" asked Theodora hopefully. "Can I have it?"

On Tuesday Mrs Kachunka brought in gingerbread squirrels, one for each child.

"Miss Kirsty made them," she said. "The lady I live with. Aren't they pretty?"

"It's against regulations. You know that, don't you?" sniffed Mrs Harries.

Thomas finished his thin Marmite sandwich.

Theodora picked up his gingerbread squirrel. "You don't want this," she said hopefully. "Do you?"

Thomas scowled. "You'll get fat," he said. "You'll blow up!"

On Wednesday Mrs Kachunka crowned each helping of rice pudding with a juicy jellied fruit. Then she walked over to the sandwich table.

"One each," she said, opening a spare box of jellies. "But remember to clean your teeth tonight."

Theodora smiled happily at Thomas. "You wouldn't want to get toothache," she said. "Would you?"

On Thursday Mrs Kachunka came round with a Chinese bowl full of chocolate raisins. She smiled at Thomas. "Have one," she said.

"No thanks," said Thomas, crumpling up his sandwich bag and stuffing it into his pocket. "I'm not eating your rubbish."

"Oh, Thomas," they all said. "That's mean! That's rude."

"I don't care," said Thomas, knocking over his glass of water.

"Oh, Thomas," they groaned.

"I'll eat his for him," offered Theodora. "Then it won't be wasted, will it?"

On Friday the chips were particularly crisp and delicious. Mrs Kachunka ladled out the leftovers and piled them into a bowl.

"No reason why the sandwich people can't finish these…"

"There's every reason," said Mrs Harries. "Food costs money. That lot haven't paid."

"But these are left over," argued Mrs Kachunka. "They'd only be thrown away."

"It's against regulations," said Mrs Harries.

"Oh, go on, dear," said the other dinner ladies. "We don't mind."

"Wow!" said the people on the sandwich table.

Thomas glared at Mrs Kachunka.

"You've got too many fingers."

"Maybe you haven't got enough," said Mrs Kachunka.

"And you've got green hairs all round your mouth."

"And you've got yellow hairs all over your head," said Mrs Kachunka. "Aren't we both funny?"

And the others all giggled.

"I'll eat your share of chips for you," offered Theodora.

But Thomas scowled.

"No you won't," he said, and he gobbled up every one.

Chapter Four

On Monday afternoon a small group of parents, led by Theodora's aunt, gathered outside Mr Carey's room.

Mr Carey opened the door.

"We have a complaint," said Theodora's aunt.

"Come in," said Mr Carey. "Then we can talk about it."

Theodora's aunt arranged herself stiffly on the edge of a chair. "It's about one of your dinner ladies," she said. "Mrs er…"

"Kachunka?"

"Bless you!" murmured some of the parents.

"I never heard such a ridiculous name in my life," declared Theodora's aunt.

Mr Carey picked up the telephone. "Is Mrs Kachunka still around? Good. Could she spare a few minutes?"

Mrs Kachunka came in with Snowball draped round her shoulders like a purring fur collar.

"You wanted to see me?"

Theodora's aunt shuddered. "Cats, too," she said. "Most unhygienic!"

"Oh dear," said Mrs Kachunka. "Off you go, love..." and Snowball dropped to the ground and pattered away.

Theodora's aunt put on her spectacles. "Blue hair," she noted. "Green whiskers. And far too many fingers! *Not* a suitable person to associate with my little niece!"

"There aren't any rules," said Mr Carey, "about the number of fingers…"

"And she messes up their food…"

"Oh, that reminds me," said Mrs Kachunka, popping a lozenge into her mouth.

Theodora's aunt pointed. "You see? Comes in with sweets. Bad for their teeth."

Then Mrs Kachunka held up the eyeglass with the mirrored handle and behind it her right eye seemed to grow and grow. Funny-coloured eyes too, thought Theodora's aunt. Must be some kind of foreigner.

"We'd like this lady removed," she said firmly. "Nothing personal, of course…"

Then the shutter in Mrs Kachunka's eye slowly opened and galaxies went whirling round Theodora's aunt.

"Ooh!" she squealed. "Oooh! Oh no! Not upside down. Most undignified…" She pulled herself together. "*Everything*," she sighed. "That makes me pretty important, doesn't it?"

"As important as a fruit-bat," murmured Mrs Kachunka, but Theodora's aunt didn't seem to hear.

"And this lady is an observer from...?" She glittered at Mr Carey. "It does make us rather privileged, doesn't it? Do the newspapers know? I'm sure my little niece would just love to have her photograph taken with you, Mrs er..."

"Kachunka."

"Bless you!"

Mrs Kachunka smiled. "What will you tell the newspapers?"

"Well, I'll say that..." But Theodora's aunt had already forgotten. "I'll say that we're most honoured to have you with us, Mrs er..." she said vaguely. She turned to the other parents. "Aren't we?"

"Well, yes." They looked puzzled. "If you say so..."

At a quarter to three, Class Five came boiling into the playground. Across the road, Theodora spotted her aunt getting into the Fiat.

"Oh no," sighed Theodora.

"What's the matter?" asked Helen.

"That's my aunt," said Theodora. "She's been to see Mr Carey. She said she was going to."

"What about?"

"What d'you think?"

"She's stupid to come in," said Thomas. "She should write him a letter. My dad's written him a letter."

"Not your superdad again," said Simon.

"What about your mum?" teased Amanda. "Can't she write?"

"She's too busy," said Thomas.

"I've seen your mum," said Theodora. "She came for you that day you weren't well. You've got a baby, haven't you?"

Thomas thumped her softly in the chest.

"Ow!" said Theodora.

"You don't know anything about my family," said Thomas.

"You hit me," said Theodora. "I'm telling!" And she ran up to Mrs Kachunka. "That boy hit me," she wailed, pointing at Thomas.

Mrs Kachunka said, "I wonder why?"

Theodora wiped her eyes with the back of her hand. "Aren't you going to do something?"

"Are you badly hurt?" asked Mrs Kachunka.

Theodora sniffled. "Yes, I am."

"Then sit down on the bench until you feel better."

And Theodora sat.

"Boys don't hit girls," she whimpered.

"But one just has," said Mrs Kachunka.

Theodora thought about that.

"Well it's not fair!" she grumbled. "It's not fair!"

Chapter Five

On Tuesday Mrs Kachunka came into the dinner hall with a robin on her head.

"Oh," people said, "he looks so real."

The robin ruffled her wings.

"Oh he *is* real. Is he your pet?"

"*She's* my friend," corrected Mrs Kachunka.

"Get that bird out of here!" snapped Mrs Harries. "What d'you think the inspectors would say?"

"Oh dear," said Mrs Kachunka. "Off you go, love..." and the robin fluttered gently through an open window.

After lunch Miss Fielding came over to

Class Five's table. She looked cross.

"Before you go outside," she said, "take a look at those plants. They're thirsty. They're drooping."

Class Five squirmed.

"Some people from this class are supposed to be watering them. Who did we choose?"

Robbie and Anna slowly put up their hands.

"And who else?"

Theodora went pink and pointed at Thomas. "Well, Thomas was the fourth one," she said. "It wasn't just us."

Miss Fielding sighed. "So what happened?"

"We forgot," said Robbie and Anna and Theodora.

"I didn't feel like it," said Thomas.

"I've had enough of these excuses," said Miss Fielding. "Get it done right now."

"Can't," said Robbie. "Got recorder practice."

"Can't," said Anna. "My mum's picking me up early. Got to go to the dentist."

"Oh, I'll do it," said Theodora virtuously. "Anyway, Thomas doesn't want to."

"Well, Thomas really ought to," said Mrs Kachunka. "Because Thomas has green fingers."

"No I haven't," said Thomas. "I washed them. Look."

Mrs Kachunka found the watering can and filled it. "Anyway, this is probably too heavy for you."

"But I'm strong," protested Thomas.

"But I'm stronger," said Theodora sweetly, standing up and flexing her muscles.

Thomas picked up the can. "I'll do it," he said. "Go out and play if you want to."

Theodora's cheeks turned very pink. "That's not fair," she said. "I offered first."

At the end of the afternoon Miss Fielding said, "I'm afraid Friday's outing to the Natural History Museum is off. We'll have to save it up until after Christmas. We need two grown-ups, and Mr Jackson's down with flu.

Unless one of your mums could give us a hand?"

"My mum works," said Amanda.

"So does mine…"

"So does mine…"

"Could my mum bring our new baby?"

"Forget it," said Miss Fielding. "We'll do it next term."

"Why not ask Mrs Kachunka?" sniggered Simon.

"She's a dinner lady," said Miss Fielding. "She'll be working."

All the same, Miss Fielding tried.

"I'm sure we can spare her," said Mrs Harries sourly.

"Oh, thank you," said Mrs Kachunka. "The Natural History Museum? What fun!"

That evening Miss Fielding told her boyfriend, "Mrs Kachunka's been teaching Class Three a song. And she's getting my lot to grow things. This afternoon she turned up with a whole basketful of bulbs."

"Light bulbs?" teased Miss Fielding's boyfriend, but she pretended she hadn't heard.

"And she's tagged each bulb with somebody's name," she said. "She's only been with us a few weeks – can't think how she remembers…"

"What's it mean," Thomas asked his mum, "if someone says you've got green fingers?"

"I can tell you about purple fingers," sighed Thomas's mum, pulling his sister's hand out of the blackberry pie.

"Can I have twenty pence?"

"What for this time?" asked Thomas's mum wearily.

"A flower pot."

"I see. And what are you going to put in it?"

"It's a secret," said Thomas.

Chapter Six

The next morning they planted the bulbs.

"What will they grow into?" asked Robbie.

"I don't know," said Miss Fielding. "Mrs Kachunka said wait and see – don't you remember?"

They began putting the pots inside a big cardboard box. Thomas dropped his.

"Oh, Thomas," said Miss Fielding. "Now you'll have to start all over again."

She helped him scoop up the earth and reset his bulb.

"We're going to put them away in a cool, dark place," she explained. "Mr Stevens is letting us use the bottom of his store cupboard – isn't that nice of him? They'll have to be watered, mind, and you'd better not forget, or your mums won't get their Christmas flowers. I'm going to need two bulb-watering people. Who'd like to do it?"

Theodora's hand shot up at once.

"Theodora. Right. And somebody else? Thomas? Oh, good. That's settled, then. Theodora and Thomas are in charge of the bulbs."

"Oh, not Thomas," groaned Simon.

"Why ever not?" said Miss Fielding. "Besides, he's got green fingers. Mrs Kachunka said so."

Just before home time that day, they talked about the outing to the Natural History Museum.

"Is Mrs Kachunka really coming?" asked Robbie.

"Of course…"

Thomas sighed, but most people looked pleased.

"So on Friday I want you all in the playground by nine o'clock sharp. And please don't bring any more than fifty pence spending money." Miss Fielding glanced out at the golden trees and the cold blue sky. "Hope the weather stays like this for us."

But it didn't…

On Friday the sun was a watery blob, dripping its silver over billowing clouds. The minibus arrived already freckled with rain.

"Now don't all rush," shouted Miss Fielding. "And where's Theodora?"

Theodora slammed the door of her aunt's car and came galloping down the road.

"Just in time," said Miss Fielding, "or we'd have gone without you."

Mrs Kachunka, holding a rolled umbrella, bunched up her skirts and climbed on board.

Through the windscreen of the Fiat, Theodora's aunt's friend gaped. "Good heavens!" she said. "Whatever's that?"

"Don't you know?" said Theodora's aunt. "That's an Observer. Only the best schools have them…"

Theodora sat down next to Thomas. It was the last place left.

"Had to wait for my aunt's boring old friend to turn up, didn't I?" she grumbled. "That's why I was late."

"Why d'you live with her?" asked Thomas.

"You mean, where's my mum?"

Thomas looked embarrassed.

"Well I'm *not* telling," said Theodora. "You wouldn't tell me, would you? You hit me, didn't you?"

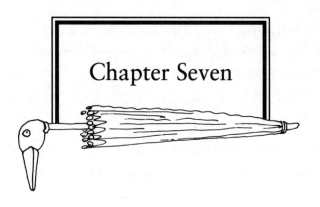

Chapter Seven

By the time they had reached the Museum it was raining steadily. They got out and huddled under umbrellas.

The driver grinned and waved at them. "Pick you up at twelve!" he called out. "Have a good morning..."

They scuttled through the big gates and across the courtyard. A security guard in a peaked cap came out through the swing doors. "Museum's closed," he said. "Come back this afternoon."

Miss Fielding looked shocked. "We can't. We've booked a coach..."

Mrs Kachunka stepped forward.

"Kachunka," she said.

The security guard grinned and shook his head. "Bless you, love. It's the damp that does it."

"So let us in, then," said Mrs Kachunka. "Quickly, or we'll all be sneezing."

"Wish I could," said the security guard. "But they're in there making this film."

"Who are?"

The security guard shrugged. "Some television lot."

Mrs Kachunka handed her umbrella to Miss Fielding. "Class Five has come to see the dinosaurs," she said, slipping seven downy fingers into her shoulder bag. "It would be a shame to disappoint them." She raised her eyeglass. "Wouldn't it?"

The security guard stared. The security guard gasped. "Cor!" he whispered. "You come a long way, missus…"

He led them through the swing doors and across the hall. "Leave those umbrellas with me," he said, spotting the trails of raindrops on the marble floor.

A young woman stepped out briskly from behind the woolly mammoth.

"Get those people out of here, Stanley. At once. The television crew has started filming." She glared at Miss Fielding. "Museum's closed," she snapped.

Mrs Kachunka raised her eyeglass.

"Oh!" sighed the woman. "Oh… " Then she looked thoughtful. "*Everything*," she murmured. "Yes I see…" She suddenly smiled at Class Five. " So what can I do for you?"

"We'd like to see the dinosaurs," said Miss Fielding.

"The dinosaurs!" shouted Class Five.

"Oh dear," said the woman. "Everyone wants to see the dinosaurs." She turned to Mrs Kachunka. "Even someone like you." She sighed. "Very well. This way."

They followed her through the deserted rooms. It was funny not to have anyone else around. No tourists. No little kids. No other school outings. Creepy.

Outside, the sky had darkened and rain lashed against the big arched windows. They could hear their shoes scraping and thudding against the polished wood floor and from somewhere upstairs, voices echoing.

A man with a luminous tie stepped over a big roll of cable, making them all jump.

"Hi, kids," he said. Then he blinked at the woman. "I thought you'd closed the place…"

"We have," she said. "These people are our guests."

"Oh, really?" The man smiled uncertainly. "Well, pleased to meet you," he said. "Have a nice day – and keep clear of our cameras."

"Of course," said Miss Fielding indignantly.

They walked on through the Insect Gallery. Robbie nudged Simon. "See that?" he whispered.

"What?"

"Those butterflies. Look!" Turquoise and orange and blue, they were fluttering like little ghosts around Mrs Kachunka's head.

"Where did they come from?"

"Out of one of those cases," said Theodora.

"Don't be stupid," said Amanda.

"They're moving. They're real..."

"Rubbish," said Simon.

"Hush," said Miss Fielding.

The woman's high heels tap-tapped somewhere ahead of them, and they hurried to catch up.

In the Small Mammals Room, Thomas was sure he saw hares leaping and foxes tumbling with their cubs. But we haven't pressed any buttons, he thought.

The woman pushed open a heavy glass door. "Giant Fossils." She yawned. "There really *are* other things to see, you know."

Chapter Eight

They stood. They stared.

"Wow!" said Robbie.

"Look at him!"

"He's *enormous*!"

The woman shrugged. "I must go and keep an eye on that television crew," she said. "Think they own the place."

Anna pointed at one of the skeletons. "Imagine," she giggled, "having him for a pet. Imagine taking him out for walks on a lead..."

"Some lead," said Simon. "A mile long."

"His neck might be small enough for a big dog collar," observed Carly.

"He's all neck," said Helen. She nudged Anna. "So what would you call him?"

Anna thought about it. "Frankie," she said. "Short for Frankenstein."

"Call him Thomas," said Simon. "All neck and no brain."

"He's got a name already," said Miss Fielding. "Look. He's called Diplodocus."

"You could call him Dippie then," said Robbie. He waved. "Hi, Dippie…"

"Hey, aren't they supposed to be skeletons?" said Simon nervously. For Diplodocus had suddenly plumped out.

"He moved," whispered Helen. "I saw him!"

"Don't be silly," said Miss Fielding. "They're only models…"

But the small, grey-brown head of Diplodocus had oozed unmistakably forward. The nostrils were twitching, the little tangerine eyes were glittering, the crocodile jaws grinned wickedly, and at the other end of the long platform, the tail twisted and lashed.

"I'm scared," whimpered Lalita.

"Well, don't be," said Miss Fielding briskly. "It's not real. It's some new kind of animation. Very convincing, though. I'm expecting some really good drawings from you lot after this."

Diplodocus began nosing at Theodora's bright Peruvian scarf. Theodora clasped it tightly round her neck.

"You leave that alone," she yelled. But Diplodocus was stronger than Theodora. He

tugged off the scarf and swung it high,
waving it from side to side.

Theodora turned scarlet. "Give it back!"
She was close to tears. "Give it back, you
stupid, horrible monster! You're not
supposed to be real – don't you know that?"

But Diplodocus had spotted some high-
growing ferns. He reached up and tore off a
bunch, and the scarf slipped from between his
jaws and dropped to the ground.

"You see?" said Mrs Kachunka. "He's a

vegetarian. You don't have to worry about him – unless you happen to be a fern…"

Theodora's scarf drooped over the edge of the platform.

"Go and get it," teased Simon, giving her a shove. "Go on. Dare you…"

"How about that one?" said Miss Fielding. "Look, he's walking about on two legs, like us – see?" She stepped forward and read out the label. "He's called an iguanodon."

"Miss – where did all the ferns come from?" asked Helen. "They weren't there when we came in…"

Thomas crept forward. He caught the end of Theodora's scarf and pulled.

"Oh, Thomas, you *are* brave," said Theodora, winding it back round her neck.

"No he's not," said Simon. "That thing wouldn't have hurt him. It's a vegetarian. She said."

"There's one with horns," said Robbie. "And a frill round its neck."

"He's a triceratops," said Mrs Kachunka.

"But look – here comes the king of them all…"

The thin, ferny trees swayed and shook as the monster reared up on its hind legs. It opened its huge mouth and roared. Its teeth were like daggers. Its claws were like knives. Class Five retreated behind a glass case.

"Tyrannosaurus," whispered Miss Fielding. "Tyrannosaurus the king…"

"And he," said Mrs Kachunka, "is *not* a vegetarian."

"Well, thank goodness he's only a skeleton," said Miss Fielding.

"He wasn't just now," said Thomas.

"And those funny fern things," said Anna. "Look, they've all gone! They're all up there in that long picture."

"That long picture's called a frieze," said Miss Fielding.

"And that's just what killed them," said Mrs Kachunka.

"What, that picture?"

Mrs Kachunka grinned. "The other kind of freeze. It got very, very cold and they all died."

"No central heating," joked Carly.

"Creatures come, creatures go," said Mrs Kachunka.

"Not people," said Simon. "People are much too clever."

"But cleverness," said Mrs Kachunka, "isn't really enough…"

Chapter Nine

In the entrance hall they lingered over cards
and posters.

"Can we buy some?" asked Thomas.

"Oh, Thomas, be reasonable," said Miss
Fielding. "They've opened the Museum
specially for us. We can't expect them to open
the shop too."

The security guard looked at Mrs
Kachunka.

"If they want to buy cards, love," he said,
"I can open the till."

"I want some pictures of those dinosaurs,"
said Robbie. "But not just skeletons. The way
we saw them."

"I don't think they've done any yet," said Miss Fielding. "That was very new."

"I'm getting a poster," boasted Simon.

"You can't," said Carly. "They're too expensive."

"Not for me," said Simon, bringing two pound coins out of his pocket.

"Oh, that's not fair!" exclaimed Theodora.

"Weren't you around," said Miss Fielding, "when I said fifty pence?" And Simon went pink.

Theodora turned to Thomas. "Aren't you buying any?"

"I don't buy cards," said Thomas. "It's silly."

Outside, the sun was lighting up the clouds.

"Ooh look!" said Carly. "A rainbow!"

They climbed back on the bus. Theodora fingered her scarf.

"Were those things real, d'you think?"

"They looked real," said Thomas. "But they couldn't have been..."

"You know what I think?" whispered Theodora.

"What?"

"I think Mrs Kachunka made it happen." She touched her scarf. "You were really brave…"

Thomas said nothing.

"My mum sent me this," said Theodora.

Thomas was silent.

"So don't you want to know? Aren't you going to ask me?"

"Ask you what?"

"About my mum."

"OK," said Thomas. "Where is she?"

"Peru," said Theodora triumphantly.

"So where's Peru?"

"South America."

"Oh," said Thomas. He thought about it. "So why's she in Peru?"

"They work there, silly. Both of them. With the World Health thing. But she's coming back for Christmas…" Theodora glared at Thomas. "There. I told you, didn't I? Go on. Your turn. You tell me."

Thomas was puzzled.

"About what?"

"About your lot. Your mum. And your baby. And your dad."

Thomas frowned. "None of your business, is it?"

"Oooh," said Theodora. "That's not fair…"

Simon was planning a bonfire party on the dump at the back of his house. By the end of the following week he'd told everyone about it. He asked Robbie and Joel. He asked Debbie and Sarah and Alex.

"You're not coming," he told Thomas.

"Don't want to," said Thomas.

Theodora's aunt was looking at a magazine.

"We ought to have a bonfire," said Theodora.

"Not in my garden," said Theodora's aunt.

Theodora slipped an arm round her aunt's shoulders.

"Well, fireworks then."

"Dreadful things!" said Theodora's aunt.

"Simon's asked Mrs Kachunka to his party," lied Theodora.

Theodora's aunt looked alarmed. "And has she accepted?"

"I don't know..." Theodora watched her aunt's face. "Simon's having sausages on sticks and baked potatoes..."

Theodora's aunt sniffed. "If I were giving a fireworks party," she said thoughtfully, "I'd do braised chicken and mushroom canapés and little mince pies. And champagne for the grown-ups. Especially if Mrs Kachunka were coming…"

"Then I'll ask her," said Theodora.

Theodora told Anna and Helen and Carly and Bhavin.

"Want to come to my fireworks party?"

"You bet…"

"Want to come to my fireworks party?" she said to Thomas.

"Can I?" said Thomas.

"I wouldn't ask you, silly," said Theodora, "if you couldn't."

Mrs Kachunka was tickling Snowball's chin.

"Mrs Kachunka…"

"Hello, Theodora."

"Will you come to my fireworks party?"

"I don't know about that," said Mrs Kachunka. "Will there be bangers?"

"Oh lots," said Theodora hopefully.

"Then I won't come. They scare me. And they frighten other creatures."

"No bangers," said Theodora quickly.
"Honest. We wouldn't have bangers."

"Is Thomas invited?"

"Course. He's my friend."

"In that case," said Mrs Kachunka,
"I'd love to."

Chapter Ten

Mr Williams next door had rubbish to burn.

"Why don't you have your party in my garden?" he suggested. "Then you could have a bonfire too."

"What an excellent idea," said Theodora's aunt, thinking of her neat flower-beds.

"After all," she boasted to Mrs Williams, "not many of us get the chance to entertain someone like Mrs Kachunka."

"What's so special about her?" asked Mrs Williams.

But Theodora's aunt had already forgotten.

"I can't spend my precious time gossiping," she said.

Theodora's aunt made mince pies and canapés. She made sausage rolls and gingerbread men and marzipan dates and chocolate slices. Soon the deep-freeze was bulging.

"The dinner hall looks like a jungle these days," said Miss Fielding. "Well done to the plant waterers!"

"It wasn't just us," said Anna. "It was Mrs Kachunka. She did things…"

"What kinds of things?"

Anna wriggled. "Dunno. She sort of – fiddled. Thomas did too…"

"Well, Thomas has green fingers," said Miss Fielding, "so that isn't surprising."

"Show us your green fingers, then," sniggered Simon in the playground.

"Oh shut up, Simon!" said Alex. "Bet you can't make things grow."

"That what it means?" Thomas whispered to Theodora.

"Didn't you know?"

"Course I did," said Thomas. "I just forgot."

"My dad's bought twenty-five rockets," boasted Simon. "And two big boxes of bangers."

"We can't have bangers," said Theodora sweetly. "Mrs Kachunka doesn't like them." She turned to Thomas. "Bring your mum," she said. "We've got mountains of food. Bring your baby too."

"Thanks," mumbled Thomas.

"Who's got a girlfriend?" chanted Simon.

"You're stupid," said Robbie. "Anyway, their lot's got Mrs Kachunka."

When he got home, Thomas slipped persuasive fingers round his mum's neck. "Can you?" he pleaded. His mum's tired face made a little smile.

"Well, you can't come all the way back by yourself," she said. "But I'll have to bring Julie."

"They said that's OK."

Thomas's mum shook her head. "She'll scream," she said. "She'll yell. I know she will. Those friends of yours don't know what they're letting themselves in for…"

Next evening, Thomas's mum brushed out Julie's curls and pinned them back with two ladybird clips.

"We're going to a party," she explained. "And you've got to be a good girl."

Julie pouted. "No," she said. "Won't."

They arrived at seven.

"Oh isn't she sweet?" said Theodora. "Aren't you lucky? Wish I had a sister."

"I'd rather have a puppy," said Thomas.

"What a dear little thing," said Theodora's aunt. She turned to Mrs Kachunka. "*Do* try one of my canapés…"

Mrs Kachunka popped a silver lozenge into her mouth.

"I have a special diet," she said.

Theodora's aunt shook her head disbelievingly. "But you're so slim," she wailed.

Soon the bonfire was crackling and fireworks were swishing in fountains of green and pink and gold.

"Oooh!" they said. "Oooh!"

"More!" squealed Julie. "More! More!"

"That's it, I'm afraid," said Mr Williams, too soon. "This last box won't light. Must have got damp."

"Try some of mine," offered Mrs Kachunka.

Mr Williams peered at the four transparent pyramids nestling inside a large matchbox.

"Those aren't fireworks?" he said.

Mrs Kachunka nodded.

"No instructions," said Mr Williams.

"Just push them into that flower-bed."

"So how do you light them?"

"You don't…"

People were thinking that the show was over when the first thin stems of violet, orange, crimson and vanilla went shooting across the sky.

"Oh!" they gasped. "Oh!"

"Wow!" said Thomas.

"Lasers," breathed Carly. "Super-lasers."

"Magic," whispered Theodora. "And I know who did it…"

The stems grew shoots and the shoots grew flowers – spirals of glittering pink and

turquoise, scallops and frills of sparkly
rainbows and vast emerald starbursts that
spread across the sky.

"Ooh!" they sighed. "Ooh..."

Julie blinked. Then she wriggled out of her
mum's arms and slipped sticky fingers into
Theodora's hand.

Theodora was thrilled.

"Hey, look!" she said. "Your little girl likes
me..."

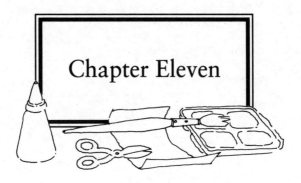

Chapter Eleven

By the end of November most of the bulbs were showing green points.

"We should bring them out now," said Miss Fielding, "and watch them grow."

They stood them on the models shelf, where it was shadowy and cool. "They've got to get used to the light," explained Miss Fielding. "We don't want to shock them."

The classroom was particularly bright and colourful. They'd stuck pictures of the two firework parties over big sheets of black paper. They'd made mobiles out of conkers and leaves and they'd pinned up their dinosaur frieze.

Anna had painted a diplodocus.

"I liked him best," she said.

"I didn't," said Theodora.

Robbie did two triceratops fighting.

Thomas had cut ferns from green tissue and
fixed them to spindly tree-trunks.

"Brilliant!" said Theodora.

"If you can do work like that," said Miss Fielding, "I'll expect wonders from you next term."

Simon drew Tyrannosaurus the King. "Watch out, Thomas!" he said. "He's coming to get you…"

"Funny thing about that animation," said Miss Fielding. "Museum doesn't seem to know anything about it."

"It was those film people," said Carly.

"It was Mrs Kachunka," said Theodora. "She did it."

"Nonsense," said Miss Fielding.

Theodora found Mrs Kachunka.

"That time in the Museum…" she began, rubbing the toe of her shoe against the surface of the playground.

"It was fun, wasn't it?" said Mrs Kachunka.

Theodora took a deep breath. "It was you," she said. "You made them come real…"

Mrs Kachunka smiled. "What's real?"

"Oh *you* know," said Theodora.

She wandered over to Thomas. "When can I come to your house?"

"Haven't got a house."

"Well your what's-it then..."

"I told you," said Thomas. "You can't."

"You always say that," grumbled Theodora. "It's not fair. I asked you to my party..."

"It's too far."

"We could go on the bus. You do, don't you? And my aunt could pick me up later."

"I told you," said Thomas. "No."

"You're mean," said Theodora. "You're rotten. I'm sick of you. I'm not your friend any more," and she went back to Mrs Kachunka.

Mrs Kachunka had Snowball on her lap.

"Kittens," she announced, and her downy fingers curled and flexed with pleasure. "Just two." She stood up, cradling the cat. Then she placed her tenderly on the ground.

"They'll be ready in time for the New Year."

"How d'you know?" asked Robbie.

"Don't know much, do you?" said Simon.

"I want one," said Helen. "I'm going to ask my mum."

Anna bent down and felt Snowball's tummy. "She's not very fat," she said. "Are you sure?"

Mrs Kachunka smiled. "We females always know these things," she said, bending down and stroking Snowball's ear.

Mrs Kachunka walked over to Thomas. "Would you like a kitten?"

"No," snapped Thomas.

"Why not?"

"Don't like kittens," said Thomas. "Don't like cats."

"You like Snowball," said Mrs Kachunka.

Thomas went pink. "Can't have one," he mumbled. "No babies, no pets. That's the rule."

"Whose rule?"

"Mr Buckley. Our landlord."

"He can't make rules like that," protested Helen.

"Yes, he can," said Thomas. "It's his house. He tried to throw us out once, when Mum had my sister, but our social worker stopped him."

"Get your famous dad to tackle him," teased Simon.

"He has," said Thomas. "My dad's bigger than him. Gave him a bashing. Put him in hospital."

"Oh sure, sure," said Simon.

Mrs Kachunka took something out of her bag.

"What's that?" said Theodora.

"May I come to your flat, Thomas?" asked Mrs Kachunka.

"No, you can't," said Thomas.

"Aren't you rude?" said Theodora.

Mrs Kachunka raised her eyeglass.

"Oooh!" gasped Thomas.

For when Thomas stared back at Mrs Kachunka, galaxies went spinning around his head.

He grew a tail. He had wings. He grew a beak and ate a worm. Then he was the worm and the grass blades were as high as trees. Then leaves sprouted from behind his ears and flowers budded from the tips of each finger and a voice said, "*You are everything, Thomas. Everything. Everything...*"

"What, me?" said Thomas.

Mrs Kachunka put away her eyeglass.

"I like your mum," she said. "And your baby sister. May I come and visit you?"

Thomas gulped. "OK," he said reluctantly. "You win."

"Then that's all arranged," said Mrs Kachunka. "Last day of term. After the concert." She grinned. "You'll need someone to help you with your bulb pot."

"What, that thing?" said Thomas. "I can carry that."

"Not with a flower in it."

"Can I come?" said Theodora.

"But you're not his friend," said Mrs Kachunka. "You said so."

Theodora looked embarrassed.

"Didn't mean it. Honest."

"Then Thomas will have to invite you."

"You can come," said Thomas ungraciously.

"Oh goody," said Theodora. She turned to Mrs Kachunka. "My aunt could pick us both up. Where d'you live, Thomas?"

"Derwent Road. Number forty-three. Basement," said Mrs Kachunka. "That's where Thomas lives."

Thomas's mouth fell open. "How did you know?"

"There goes the bell," said Mrs Kachunka. "Run along, both of you…"

Chapter Twelve

Helen asked, "Can we have one of your kittens, Mr Stevens?"

"What kittens?"

"Your cat's having kittens," said Carly. "Didn't you know?"

Mr Stevens gently prodded Snowball's tummy. "I believe you're right," he said. "You lot must be psychic."

"Can we have a kitten?" Theodora asked her aunt.

"Certainly not."

"Why?"

Theodora's aunt shuddered.

"It would scratch my upholstery."

"I could train it not to."

"You can't train a cat," Theodora's aunt said firmly.

By the second week of December the bulbs were ready to be moved into the light. They were growing fast. Simon's already had a long fleshy stem.

"Bet you mine's a hyacinth," said Helen.

"Bet you mine's a tulip…"

"I think mine's going to be a gladioli," said Simon. He giggled. "Have you seen Thomas's?"

The pebbly thing with the blue-green fronds did not look impressive.

"What's that supposed to be?" asked Robbie.

"Dunno," said Thomas.

"It's just slow," said Miss Fielding. "You'll have to be patient."

At playtime Thomas looked for Mrs Kachunka.

"That bulb you gave me..."

"Don't worry," she said. "It'll grow."

By the end of the week they'd begun practising for the Christmas concert. Class Five was singing a round. Thomas kept coming in at the wrong place.

"Oh, Thomas," said Miss Fielding. "Concentrate. Do."

After school they hung about in the playground.

"Your mum coming?" Theodora asked Thomas.

"She can't. She's got Julie."

Simon said, "Can't she get a babysitter?"

"She can bring Julie," said Carly. "My baby brother's coming."

"She'll yell," said Thomas. "She always does."

"You should hear my brother," said Carly.

"Your superdad coming?" teased Simon.

"No," said Thomas quickly. "He's working."

"Mine's taking time off," said Simon virtuously.

Robbie groaned. "Your dad, your dad," he said to Simon. "He's a real goody-goody, isn't he?"

Chapter Thirteen

Nobody knew who started the story.

Helen whispered it.

Then Anna told Lalita.

"It's not true, is it?" said Theodora.

"Don't go," said Anna, tearfully. "I won't let you."

"I have to," said Mrs Kachunka.

"But why?" wailed Theodora.

"I'm only here for a while."

"You mean the council?" said Robbie.

"Something like that…"

"Then we'll write to them," said Robbie, "and we'll all sign the letter. We'll make them keep you…"

"Bet it was Mrs Harries," said Simon.

Theodora spoke to her aunt.

"After the concert," she said, "I'm going over to Thomas's house. Mrs Kachunka's coming too. Could you pick us up afterwards?"

"Is it true what they say about Mrs Kachunka?"

"That she's leaving?" said Theodora bleakly. "Yes."

"But she can't!" protested Theodora's aunt. "I was going to get her to speak at my Club..."

By the beginning of the last week of term, the first buds had begun to open.

Helen got her hyacinth. Oh, what a hyacinth!

There were tulips and irises and the biggest daffodils anyone had ever seen.

"If we put them in a flower show," said Miss Fielding, "they'd all win first prize!"

Thomas's pebbly thing had pushed up into

a big oval with a crack at the top.

Simon poked at it with the top of a pencil.

"Weird," he muttered. "Weird."

Simon's big plant was almost the last one to open.

"That's not a gladioli," shouted Simon crossly.

"It's an onion," giggled Robbie. Robbie's dad kept an allotment, so Robbie knew. "Simon's got an onion flower."

Theodora smelt it and pulled a face. "Pooh!" she said. "Pooh!"

"Nothing wrong with onions," said Miss Fielding. "And they make very pretty flowers when they go to seed."

"It's better than Thomas's," said Simon.

"Thomas's is just slow," Miss Fielding said. "It'll probably come out in the holidays. I'll get Mr Stevens to keep an eye on it."

"You can have this one if you like," offered Simon.

At pudding time on the day of the concert a timid old lady tiptoed nervously into the dinner hall.

"She got me to come," she apologized, pointing at Mrs Kachunka.

Mrs Kachunka slipped seven downy fingers round the old lady's shoulders.

"This is Miss Kirsty," she said. "The lady I've been living with. Miss Kirsty used to be a cook in a big house. It was Miss Kirsty who made you the gingerbread squirrels and the treacle fudge and the almond pies. And just look what she's brought you today..."

Then two dinner ladies wheeled in a trolley with a huge snowball cake spiked all over with sparklers.

"Ooh!" they all said, and they started to clap.

Miss Kirsty's cheeks became very pink and she tried to hide behind Mrs Kachunka's cape.

"Had to cancel their Christmas puds for this," complained Mrs Harries. "Lot of silly nonsense, if you ask me."

"But nobody has, dear," said the other dinner ladies.

Chapter Fourteen

Playtime was short that day. People went back early to their classrooms to get ready for the concert.

Class Five's room looked odd. Different. There was a soft light. A radiance.

"Somebody's switched something on," said Miss Fielding. "But what?"

Then she saw.

"Oh!" she gasped. "Oh!"

"Wow!" said Helen. "What is it?"

For out of Thomas's pebble had sprung a flower. Its white winged petals were awash with rainbows. Its golden stamens glowed.

"Oh, Thomas!" said Theodora.

"Oh, Thomas!" said Anna."

"She said he had green fingers," said Miss Fielding. "She was right."

"That thing's not real," said Simon.

"Could work off batteries," said Carly thoughtfully.

"Touch it," said Thomas. "Go on. Touch it."

So Simon did.

"Oh," he said in a very small voice. "Oh..."

At half past three they arranged themselves in the hall, the infants on one side and the juniors on the other.

Out in the playground, Thomas's mum hovered shyly on the edge of the crowd, Julie hiding behind her coat.

"How good to see you," said Theodora's aunt. She peeped round at Julie. "Who's a pretty girl, then?" Julie stuck out her tongue.

"Ooh, naughty!" scolded Thomas's mum.

They went inside. The wooden chairs scraped as they all sat down. Simon's dad was still wearing his business suit. Mr Carey got up and said things but nobody listened. Then the concert started.

There were recorders and violins and drums. The infants sang a carol, and some of the Indian girls, in their best saris, did a festive dance. People loved it. They clapped and clapped.

Mrs Kachunka came on with a funny-looking stringed thing. "It's a sort of multiple harp," she explained, holding it up for them all to see. "For people like me, who've got too many fingers..."

Class Three came over, shuffling and giggling, and arranged itself behind her.

"This is our secret, isn't it?" said Mrs Kachunka, and they nudged each other: "Yes!"

Mrs Kachunka played a fourteen finger chord.

"We're going to sing you a song about your planet," she said. "Beautiful Planet Earth..."

Some of the parents were whispering.

"Funny colour skin..."

"Amazing hair..."

"I thought she was just a dinner lady..."

When Class Five stood up to sing its round, Thomas looked out for his mum. He was so busy looking that he came in at the wrong place again, but Julie was yelling so nobody noticed.

Chapter Fifteen

The minute the concert was over Class Five rushed to show off its flowers.

"What a magnificent tulip!" said Theodora's aunt.

"It's for you," said Theodora. "Please take it. It's very heavy..."

"What a wonderful hyacinth!" said Helen's mum. "Aren't you clever?"

"Not as clever as Thomas," said Helen.

Simon's dad wrinkled his nose. "Doesn't smell very flowery."

Thomas's mum timidly touched the rainbowed petals of the butterfly flower. "Cor!" she said. "What is it?"

"Dunno," said Thomas, looking at the cracked varnish on her bitten-back nails.

"Well, it's gorgeous!" she said. "I've never seen anything like it."

"It's for Dad," whispered Thomas. "D'you think they'll let him have it?"

"Doubt it," said Thomas's mum. "But he may be coming out for a few days soon…"

Free of her tulip, Theodora came skipping across the playground.

"I'm ready," she chirped.

"Right," said Mrs Kachunka. "Let's be off then."

They got out at the bus stop next to the football ground and turned into a road full of big shabby houses. They walked past four dustbins and down some cracked concrete steps. Thomas's mum unlocked the door.

"It's nothing grand," she said. "It's a dump, really."

She switched on the light.

"Oh, Mum!" said Thomas, when he saw

the pretty biscuits, the crisps, the Smarties in a little glass bowl and the jug of orange squash.

"Well it's not often we have visitors," said Thomas's mum. "Thomas, put that gorgeous plant in the middle. There. Ooh isn't it shiny? Better than a table lamp..."

Theodora looked at the scratched telly and the rust-stained fridge.

"Where's your room?" she asked Thomas. "And who sleeps down there?" she said, looking at the bed made up on the floor.

"Let's have some tea," said Thomas's mum.

"It's a *lovely* tea," said Mrs Kachunka. "But I have a special diet..."

"Well, I don't," said Theodora, helping herself to crisps and Smarties.

Thomas's mum poured out two glasses of orange squash.

Thomas fell silent. It had all been a mistake, he thought. He hadn't asked Theodora. She'd invited herself. And as for Mrs Kachunka, she'd *done* something to him. He watched her, squatting on the floor, letting

Julie scramble all over her.

"Tell me when you've had enough," said Thomas's mum. "She's not usually like that with strangers."

Julie grabbed at something and pulled. "Tail! Tail!" she squealed, and Thomas's mum went scarlet.

"Leave Mrs Kachunka alone!"

"Julie says she's got a *tail*!" Theodora whispered.

"It can't be real," Thomas whispered back.

"Talking about tails," said Mrs Kachunka, setting Julie down. "Mr Stevens will be giving Thomas a kitten."

Thomas's mum looked startled.

"But he can't have one. Not here. Thomas knows that. No babies, no pets. We'd be thrown out."

Mrs Kachunka took Thomas's mum's hand. "Would *you* like a kitten?"

Thomas's mum looked wistful. "You bet. Wasn't allowed pets when I was little…"

"Me want kitten," sang Julie. "Kitten. Kitten…"

Chapter Sixteen

Suddenly they heard a key scraping in the lock.

"Oh no," said Thomas's mum. "It can't be. Not now…"

The door was thrown open. Thomas's mum looked flustered. "Oh, Mr Buckley," she said. "I've got visitors…"

The plump man in the shiny leather jacket sat down at the table and helped himself to a crisp.

"Not what I'd call visitors," he said. He lit a cigarette and blew a cloud of smoke into Mrs Kachunka's face. "How about my rent?"

"But I've told you already…" Thomas's

mum sounded quite weepy. "My money hasn't come through yet."

Mr Buckley leaned over and peered at Thomas's plant.

"Pretty flower, that… Must have cost quite a bit."

"Thomas grew it," said Thomas's mum nervously.

"And pigs can fly," sneered Mr Buckley. Under the table, Julie stuck out her tongue.

Mrs Kachunka reached for her bag.

"That's the idea," said Mr Buckley approvingly. "Off you go, madam. No freaks in here. I run a high class establishment."

Mrs Kachunka drew out her eyeglass. "Kachunka," she said.

"And you can take all those nasty germs with you," said Mr Buckley, fanning himself with his newspaper.

Mrs Kachunka raised her eyeglass.

"Mr Buckley," she said, and her right eye seemed to grow and grow.

Mr Buckley blinked. Mr Buckley gaped.

"Fancy tricks," he mumbled, fingering his gold earring.

Mrs Kachunka ran seven downy fingers over peeling wallpaper.

"Mr Buckley," she said. "Would *you* like to live in a place like this?" And the shutter in her right eye slowly opened.

Mr Buckley gawped.

"Fix this place," ordered Mrs Kachunka. "A lady can't bring up her young in a dump like this."

"She's no lady," said Mr Buckley, and he pointed a quivering finger at Thomas. "His dad's in jail."

"Mr Buckley," said Mrs Kachunka, "*you* should be in jail!"

Mr Buckley looked hurt. "But I'm an honest man."

"And I'm the queen of the fairies!" said Mrs Kachunka. And galaxies went spinning round Mr Buckley's head.

Mr Buckley felt faint. "I must be getting the flu," he moaned, dropping his cigarette into

Theodora's orange squash.

And the ground cracked. The sun blazed.
A barefoot peasant looked up at him with
hungry eyes.

"Pay up," said Mr Buckley. "I want my
rent."

Then Mr Buckley's own stomach swelled
with hunger, and the dried mud scratched
against the soles of his feet.

"Ouch!" protested Mr Buckley. "That's not
fair!"

A starving dog came sniffing at his ankles.

Mr Buckley picked up a stick. "Not fair!"
he shouted. *Thwack! Thwack!* That made
him feel better.

But Mr Buckley *was* the dog and his back was stinging from his own beating. "Not fair," he mouthed, but he could only yelp. And the voice said, "*You are everything, Mr Buckley. Everything. Everything…*"

Mr Buckley nibbled at the flea that was biting his paw, but Mr Buckley *was* the flea. "Help!" he screamed. But his voice made no sound.

Mrs Kachunka lowered her eyeglass. "Make this place fit to live in," she said. "Or you could be a head louse…"

Mr Buckley shivered.

"And make proper arrangements for the kitten."

Mr Buckley gulped. "What kitten?"

"Why, Thomas's kitten. It'll need a cat door…"

"No babies, no pets," croaked Mr Buckley.

"You'd make a very tasty mouse," said Mrs Kachunka, flexing each one of her fourteen fingers.

Mr Buckley stepped hastily backwards.

"Cat food costs money," he muttered.

"Oh, Thomas will see to that," said Mrs Kachunka. "You see, Thomas is going to win the Kitkat prize…"

"Whatever's that?" said Theodora.

"It's a raffle. Free cat food. For ever." Mrs Kachunka smiled. "And Thomas will have the winning number."

"How d'you know?" said Thomas.

"By looking…"

Mr Buckley was scratching his head thoughtfully.

"We should go into business, you and me," he said, grabbing a fistful of Smarties and stuffing them into his mouth. "We could make millions…"

Then Mrs Kachunka picked up Mr Buckley and shook him.

"Think of the good we could do," gibbered Mr Buckley, chocolate dribbling down his chin.

"You can do some good right now," said Mrs Kachunka. "By keeping your promises. And you know what will happen to you if you don't?"

Mr Buckley nodded.

"You see, you are *everything*, Mr Buckley. Do try to understand. Thomas does." She dropped him. "You may go now."

"Thank you," whispered Mr Buckley.

"And in future, knock before walking into someone's flat. Your manners are atrocious!"

Thomas's mum gulped back a mouthful of cold tea. "What did you do to Mr Buckley?" she whispered.

"I made him feel…"

Julie crawled out from under the table. "Kitten," she said. "Now."

Thomas's mum sighed. "He won't keep his word," she said. "He never does."

"I think he will," said Mrs Kachunka, "this time…"

Theodora was curious. "What did your dad *do*?" she blurted.

"Thomas's dad made a mistake," explained Mrs Kachunka. "People do. He won't let it happen again."

Theodora looked ashamed. "Sorry, Thomas. I shouldn't have asked."

Thomas's mum gave Mrs Kachunka a big hug. "You're ever so nice," she said. "And I don't care *how* many fingers you've got. Come again. Come any time."

"When my aunt turns up," said Theodora, "will you make her let *us* have a kitten?"

"That wouldn't be fair," said Mrs Kachunka. "Your aunt doesn't like cats."

"But I do," said Theodora.

"You can share mine if you like," said Thomas.

There was a knock at the door. Thomas's mum sighed. "He's back…"

"Bet it's my aunt," grumbled Theodora. "She always comes early."

The figure on the doorstep was gaunt and shadowy. "Kachunka," it said.

"Bless you," said Thomas's mum.

"It's for me," said Mrs Kachunka. "I ordered a taxi."

"But we were going to take you home," protested Theodora.

"You really going?" said Thomas's mum.

"I must."

"We'll never forget you…"

"You'd better," said Mrs Kachunka. "Or I *will* be in trouble." She turned briskly to Thomas. "If you look after that flower," she said, "it might keep until New Year."

Thomas tried to follow them up the steps but a loud clap of thunder sent him scuttling back.

"Storm starting," said his mum, peering up at the sky. "Mrs Kachunka got away just in time…"